The Little Buggers
Insect & Spider Poems

J. Patrick Lewis pictures by Victoria Chess

Dial Books for Young Readers New York

Published by Dial Books for Young Readers
A member of Penguin Putnam Inc.
375 Hudson Street
New York, New York 10014

Text copyright © 1998 by J. Patrick Lewis
Pictures copyright © 1998 by Victoria Chess
Typography by Amelia Lau Carling
Printed in Hong Kong
First Edition
10 9 8 7 6 5 4 3 2 1

Library of Congress Cataloging in Publication Data
Lewis, J. Patrick.
The little buggers: insect and spider poems /
by J. Patrick Lewis; pictures by Victoria Chess.
p.   cm.
ISBN 0-8037-1769-5.—ISBN 0-8037-1770-9 (lib. bdg.)
1. Insects—Juvenile poetry. 2. Spiders—Juvenile poetry.
3. Children's poetry, American. [1. Insects—Poetry.
2. Spiders—Poetry. 3. American poetry.]
I. Chess, Victoria, ill. II. Title.
PS3562.E9465L58 1998 811'.54—dc20 94-31900 CIP AC

*The artwork was rendered in watercolor and with Pelikan sepia,
which is no longer available in the United States.*

Once again for Beth, Matt, and Leigh Ann,
with love
J.P.L.

For Richard
and Norman, with love
V.C.

The Love Song of the Rhinoceros Beetle

After slugs have slimed a garden,
After watching aphids chew . . .
Rhino, dear, I beg your pardon—
What a treat to look at you!

Red Assassin Bugs disgust me,
Worms are not my cup of tea.
Which is just to say, dear, trust me,
I prefer your company.

Just when I think I could settle
For any bug of the beetle race,
Oh, I recall that heavy metal
In the middle of your face!

The Doodlebug Song

Doodlebugs are in a muddle
On the Mississippi Puddle,
Singing *hey-doodle-doodle,*
It's a Doodlebug song.
Why do Doodlebugs dawdle
And diddle in the puddle?
Where oh where
Does a Doodle belong?

Do we fly away to Ioway
Along the Io-highoway?
Or does a little Doodle boy
Hitch a ride to Illinois?
Some Doodle boys are thinkin'
Might be nice in the Land o' Lincoln,
Some Doodle girls were born
Over there in the Land o' Corn.

Doodlebugs are in a muddle
On the Mississippi Puddle,
And they don't much care to dawdle
Or to paddle to the shore.
When the Doodlebug caboodle
Hits the Highoway to Ioway,
The Doodle he won't dawdle anymore.

Insect Inspector (A Counting-Out Rhyme)

Firefly, firefly, who killed Jack Shadow?
Click beetle, quick, beetle! Find me a clue.
Weevil, boll weevil, where *were* you this evening?
Luna moth, luna moth, was he with *you*?

Ladybug, shady bug, let's hear it, sister.
Bumblebee, mumblebee, what did you see?
Katydid Katy did not have an alibi.
Centipede Speedy-o? Bring him to me.

Eavesdropper Grasshopper, answer this riddle:
Leopard moth? Peppered moth? One of them lied!
Bluebottle, you, Bottle, better know something. . . .
I'm Insect Inspector, **INSECTICIDE**.

A Streetlight in July

I am the Light on Baker Street,
The Beacon Club where Insects meet.

My customers stay out all night—
Moths and mosquitoes hanging tight

Around the suffocating heat
Of Beacon Club on Baker Street.

High fliers, fluttering about
Too carelessly, can get burned out

At Beacon Club, my all-night dive,
Where Bugs would die to stay alive.

How the Yellow Jacket Lost Her Shyness

The King of England
Once was stung
Upon his royal bottom,
And you could hear
A yellow jacket
Yell, "Oh, boy, I got 'im!"

And that is how the yellow jacket
Finally lost her shyness,
And how the English
Came to call the King
"His Royal *High*ness!"

Vegetarian Spider

On the tropical isle of Grenada,
A tarantula said, "I have made a
    Decision to eat
    Vegetables without meat,
So *please* do not pass the cicada!"

Mayfly and June Bug

Once I saw a Mayfly
Fluttering in the sun,
    As if to say,
    This must be May!
But April'd just begun.

And when I met a June Bug
Clicketing in the clover,
    He gave a nod,
    And that was odd,
July was almost over.

The Pond Glider

Damselfly
    on wings of veins
    minutely shattered windowpanes

        Damselfly
            can tilt and roll
            on automatic cruise control

Damselfly
    aboard a yacht
    of duckweed or forget-me-not

        Damselfly
            her motor hums
            all summer long to bullfrog drums

Damselfly
    who found my finger
    . . . linger

Groundwork

Nudging the day along,
a miniature infantry of Ants
marches through finger-comb grass.
Up from the country subway, they pass
Cricket and friends.

> *Beautiful song, Crickito!* they say.
> *Ah, cousins,* he replies.

Clouds bigger than cities hurry out to sea.
Anyone else would have noticed them,
but Ants are so busy—
the meadow-made world
over their shoulders—
nudging the day along.

School Lesson

God made the lowly termite
    As a warning and a sign
That kids should eat their vegetables
    Instead of knotty pine—

For what befell the termite
    Could quite easily befall
The kid who chews his pencil
    Till no pencil's left at all.

In Books Are Bugs

In books are bugs
and nothing's worse
for picture books
or books of verse—

a million micro-
scopic mites
nibbling witty,
bitty bites.

It takes them cen-
turies to do
lunch on a paper-
back or two.

Digesting pages
bit by bit,
those little buggers
never quit.

So check it out,
and listen, man—
keep on reading
while you can.

The Stinkbug and the Cricket

"Stinkbug," cried the Cricket,
"This is to remind you
  Of the many foolish friends
  Who have stood behind you!"

"What has kept you, Mrs. Locust?" said the haughty Walking Stick,

"Hear the wedding bluebells ringing? You had better make it quick!"

"But the invitation said 8 sharp!" was Mrs. L's reply.

At the
Marriage of
Black Widow
to the
Green
Bluebottle Fly

Mr. Stick and Mrs. Locust squeezed themselves into the pews.

Monarch caterpillar bridesmaids in so many pairs of shoes

Heard the Reverend Praying Mantis weep! Then all began to cry

For the Marriage of Black Widow to the Green Bluebottle Fly.

The reception was as stunning as the Royal Bug Ballet!

Daddy Longlegs caught the garter; Miss Cicada, the bouquet.

And the party of the season—no one could tell you why—

Was the Marriage of Black Widow to the Green Bluebottle Fly.

But the honeymoon was over long before the webs were cleared.

And the spider-bride was smiling—the groom had disappeared!

"Mr. Stick," said Mrs. Locust, "something always goes awry

At the Marriage of a Spider to one more Bluebottle Fly!"

Them!

The Silverfish is quite content
To build his mansion on cement
Or bathtub tile. Long after dark
He runs through Bathroom Carpet Park.

But Silverfish, beware of . . . *Them!*
They stumble in at 2 A.M.,
Turn on the light and flush the john. . . .
And some of Them have nothing on!

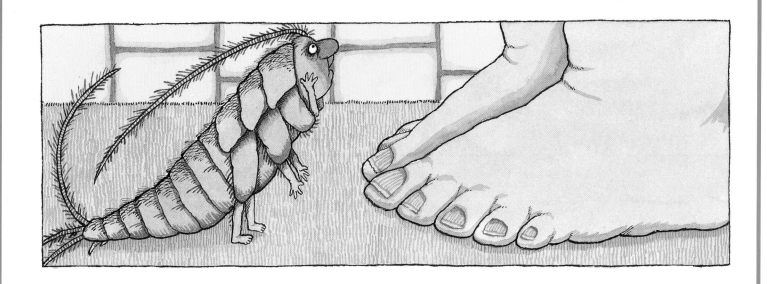

The Praying Mantis Waits

Waiting motionless for hours,
Concentrating all her powers,
She sat upon a bed of flowers—
Begonias red and yellow.

Love happened by—a handsome mate!—
Her heart began to palpitate.
She kissed him—it was their first date—
Then ate the pesky fellow.

The Marching Song of Captain Bugg

I'm Captain Bugg of the Fifth Brigade.
I'm underworked and I'm overpaid,
And I eat my toast with marmalade.
I'm Captain Bugg of the Fifth Brigade,
I'm a regular in the Army.

He's Captain Bugg, a four-star bore.
He hears a gun and he's off to war,
That's what they overpay him for.
He'll fit right in to the Officers' Corps.
He's a regular in the Army.

I'm Captain Bugg, and I spent two years
With the Horse Flyboys and the Bombardiers,
And I got my wings (behind my ears).
I'm Captain Bugg, and I spent two years
As a regular in the Army.

He's Captain Bugg, the beetle nut
Who infiltrated the Quonset hut.
Of course they'd like to fire him! But
They've gotta catch him first—hut-hut!
He's a regular in the Army!

Name Me a Butterfly

Mexican Sister, Orange-bordered Blue,
Hairstreak and Definite Patch are a few
Butterflies. They've got more nicknames by far
Than butter beans up in my grandmother's jar.

Eighty-eight, Calico, Pixie and Elf . . .
Why, I can make up a few all by myself.
Like Cinnamon Apple-crisp,
I-Do-Declare!
Miss Hildegard Tibbs with a Flower in her Hair,
Billy O',
Marty Ann,
Prince Henry's Nose,
My Lady-in-Waiting,
Old Secondhand Clothes.
As many nicknames as stars in the sky—
But one is enough. . . . Butterfly.

The Ladybug

The Ladybug wears no disguises.
She is just what she advertises:
A speckled spectacle of spring,
A fashion statement on the wing
In nature's polka dots. The thing
That often comes as some surprise is
The Ladybug wears no disguises.
She is just what she advertises:
A miniature orange kite,
A tiny dot-to-dot delight,
She envies Butterfly's excit-
Ing flutter-by! But nature's prize is
A Ladybug with no disguises,
Who is just what she advertises.

Midnight Blue or, The Cockroach's Song

My mama's name was Nightmare,
My daddy's name was Tricks.
And I was born outside a place called
Blueberry Muffin Mix.

I'm a cockroach from New Jersey!
And they call me Midnight Blue.
Free and easy living's what I do.
I'll get up to get me a late-night drink,
Cool my heels at the kitchen sink,
And before you know it, this old nose'll
Have me down the garbage disposal—
Easy living's what I do.

Well, I joined the Roaches' Union,
And I pay my union dues.
I obey the Cockroach Motto:
NEVER SLEEP IN HUMAN SHOES!
But I terrified a plumber once,
And I musta spooked a kid
'Cause I got this reputation
For the creepy things I did.

I'm a cockroach from New Jersey!
And they call me Midnight Blue.
Don't know why folks keep on bawling
Every time they see me crawling. . . .
Cockroach got to come a-calling!
Easy living's what I do.

Advice From the Scorpion

Do not be afraid, *amigo*.
Walk softly through the silent crowd
Of cactus men and cholla boys—
The touch-me-nots of the desert.
Here in scrub country,
I am a touch-me-not too—
The Land Lobster, sideways-dancing.

Do not be afraid, *amiga*.
The screaming you hear
Is only the yellow-breasted chat
Scolding the purple-mad sky.
Even in the Land of Little Rain,
Five-legged Lightning
Can break Moon's heart.

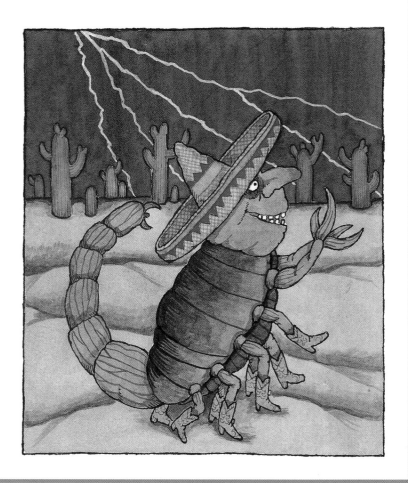

Krista Cricket

Krista Cricket, hopping madly,
Kicks her toe and breaks it badly.
Goes to visit Country Doctor,
Gets a bill that must've shocked her!

"Fifty-seven hundred dollars?!
That's an outrage!" Krista hollers.
For the rest of her reaction,
Check out Doctor Bug—in traction!

Two Spider Mites

I will meet you in June
On the garden walk.
Swift summer
Will carry me there.
For deep in the Forest
Of Broccoli Stalk,
My house is in need of repair.

When autumn decides
To let winter begin,
Spider mite,
Will you join me once more?
To keep out the cold,
We'll inquire within
At the sign of the Black Widow's door.

Who Is the Flea?

Who is the flea that barks the dog?

Who is the bee that weeps the boy?

Who is the bird that blues the sky?

Who is the moth that burns the light?

Who is the hawk corrects the wind?

Who is the worm connects the field?

Who is the ant that fields the day?

Who is the bat that grows the night?

The Almost Indestructible Last Housefly of Summer

He cannonballs
From crystal clear
Candles in
The chandelier—
PLUNK!—into
The steaming sea
Of a cup of
Instant tea!
See him prancing
Like a king
Round the table
Napkin ring.
Look at how he
Wipes his feet
On my pack of
NutraSweet!
Hear the *ZZZZZ*
Of housefly buzz?
That is what he is
   —or was!